For Nick, who makes me laugh
and gets me to try new things.—S. L. R.

STERLING CHILDREN'S BOOKS
New York

An Imprint of Sterling Publishing Co., Inc.
1166 Avenue of the Americas
New York, NY 10036

ISBN 978-1-4549-3402-8

Distributed in Canada by Sterling Publishing Co., Inc.
C/o Canadian Manda Group, 664 Annette Street
Toronto, Ontario M6S 2C8, Canada
Distributed in the United Kingdom by GMC Distribution Services
Castle Place, 166 High Street, Lewes, East Sussex BN7 1XU, England
Distributed in Australia by NewSouth Books
University of New South Wales, Sydney, NSW 2052, Australia

For information about custom editions, special sales, and premium and corporate purchases,
please contact Sterling Special Sales at 800-805-5489 or specialsales@sterlingpublishing.com.

Manufactured in China

Lot #:
2 4 6 8 10 9 7 5 3 1
12/19

sterlingpublishing.com

Design by Irene Vandervoort

The illustrations in this book were created with digital drawings
over photographs of cardboard models.

NERP!

Sarah Lynne Reul

STERLING CHILDREN'S BOOKS
New York

NERP.

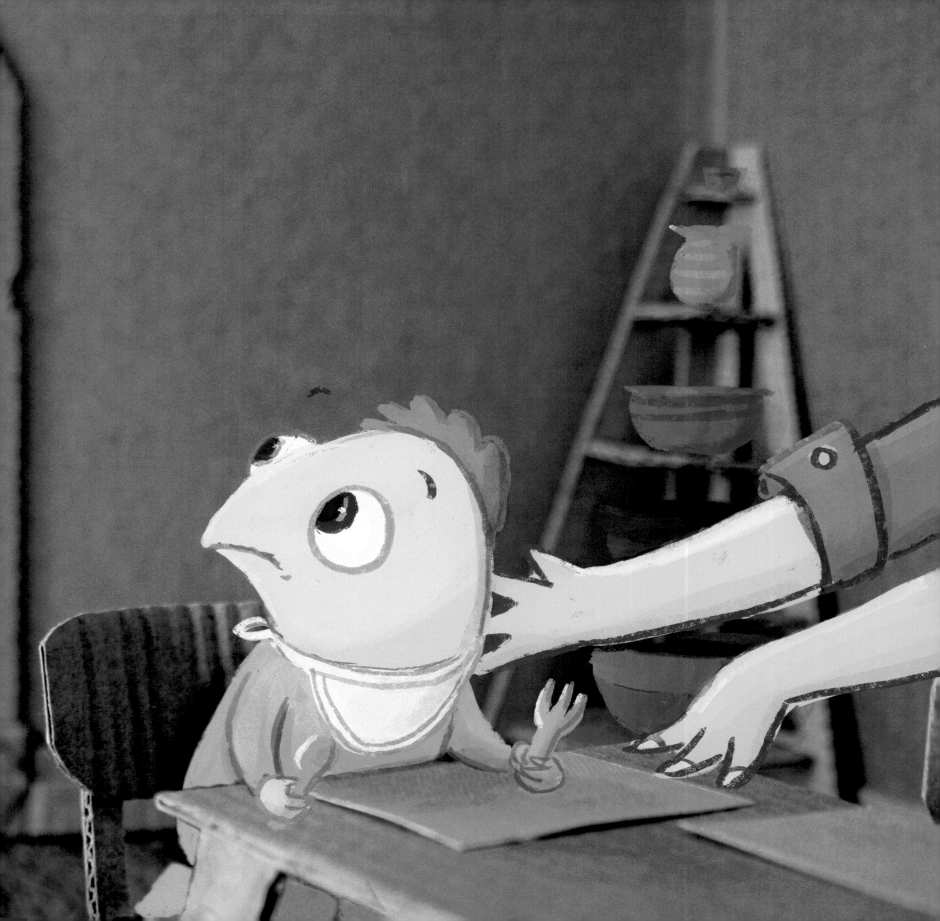

NERP.

Mushy gushy

NERPY NERP.

Slurp sluurp ssluuurrrrrrrppppp!

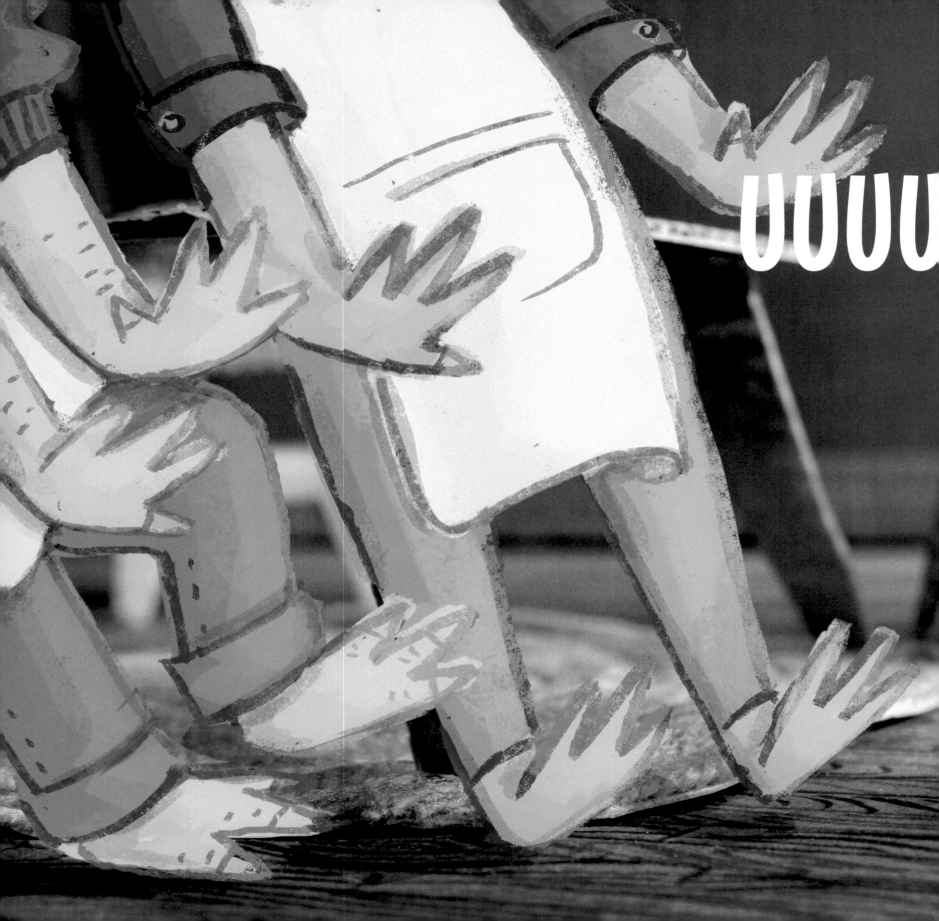

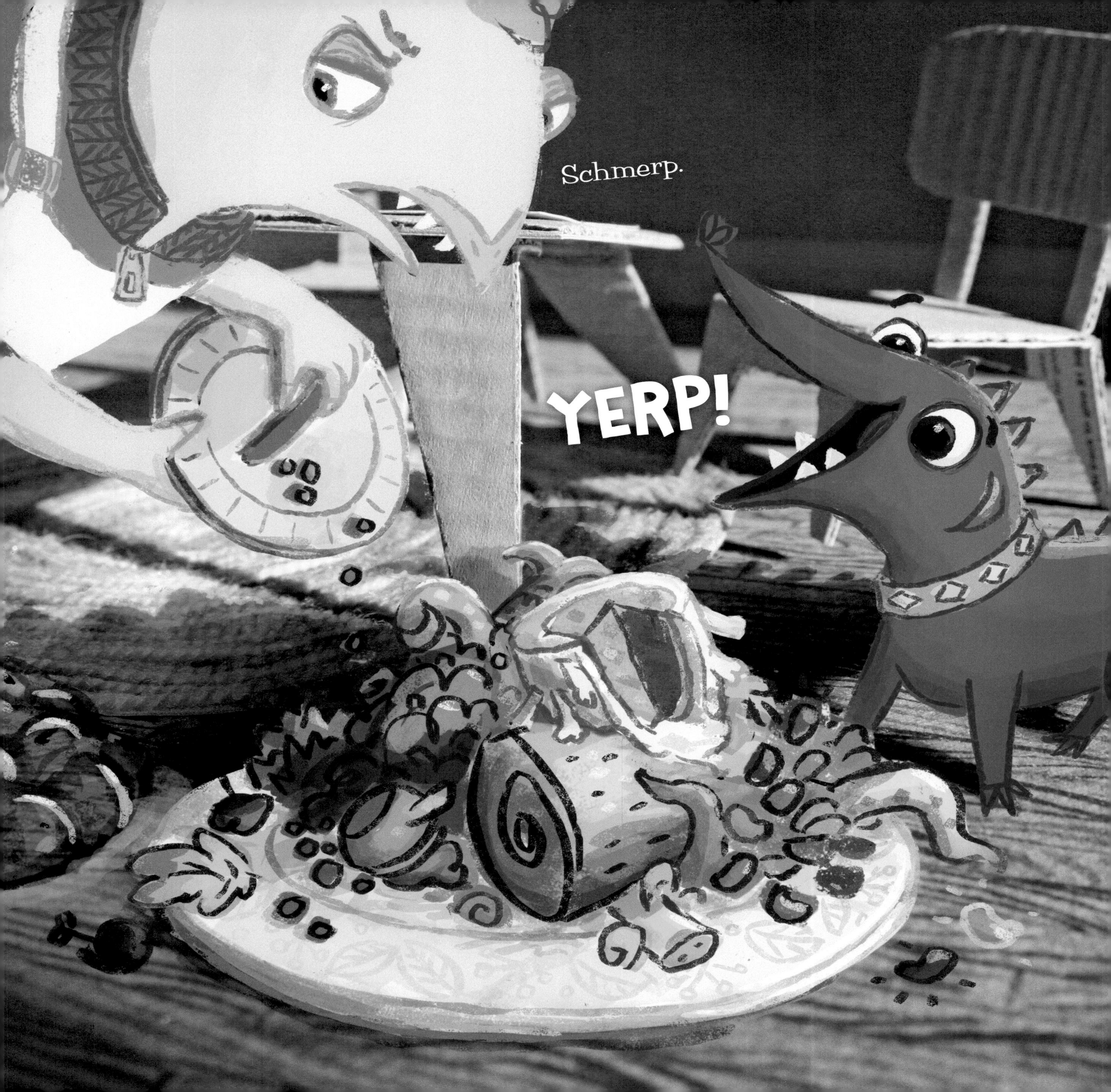
Schmerp.
YERP!

Yerpetty
yerpetty
yerpy

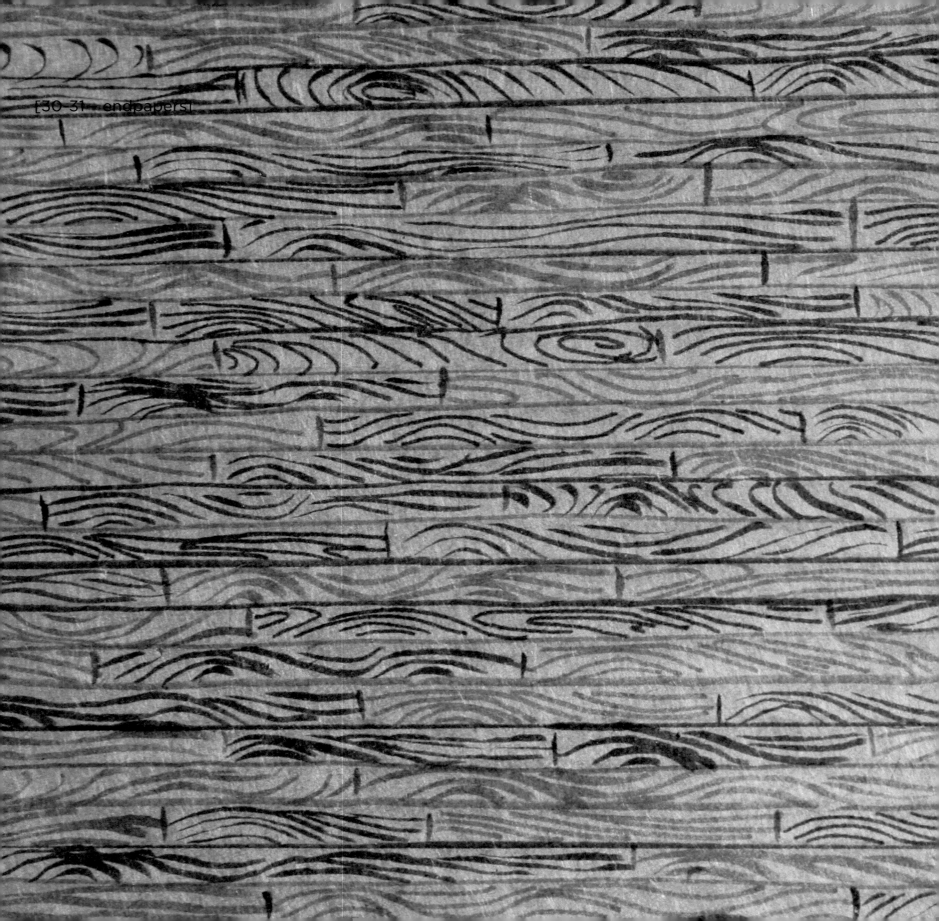